Grandpa's Angel

Jutta Bauer

Grandpa's Angel

WALKER BOOKS

AND SUBSIDIARIES

LONDON · BOSTON · SYDNEY · AUCKLAND

Grandpa always loved telling stories.

He told me stories whenever I visited him.

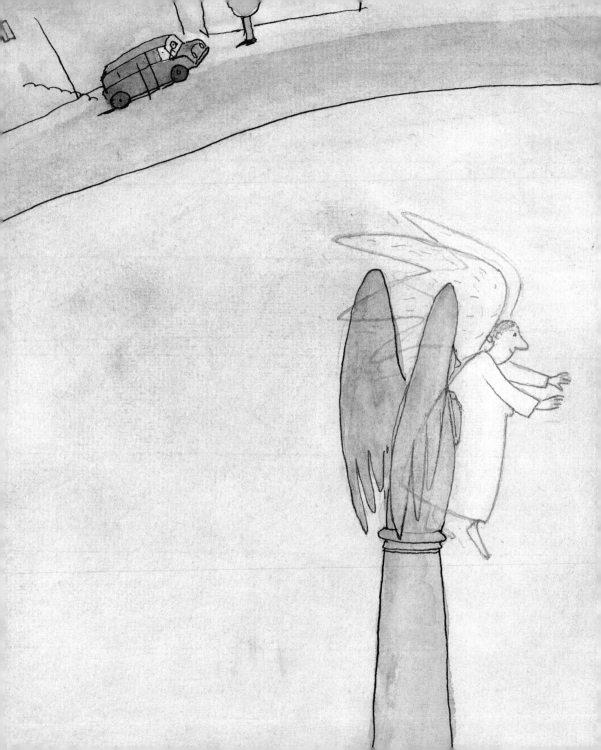

"Every morning on my way to school, I ran through the town square.

In the middle, there stood a big statue of an angel. I never stopped to look at it. I was always in a hurry and my satchel was heavy.

One day I was almost run over by a bus ...

even though there wasn't much traffic in those days.

It was a long walk to school. There were holes in the ground …

lonely street corners …

and some pretty scary geese.

But I wasn't scared. I was always the bravest...
I climbed the highest trees ...

and dived into the deepest lakes.

Even big dogs trembled in my presence.

I had my enemies, and I fought them.
Sometimes I lost …

but not often.

I was never a coward, though back then I
didn't know how dangerous times were.

My friend Joseph knew. He was frightened.
One day, he disappeared.
I never saw him again, which made me very sad.

I was growing up …

but life didn't get any easier.

There was war …

and hunger…

I did whatever jobs
I could get …

even if I wasn't very good at them.

You, with the hat!

I fell in love ...

became a father ...

built a house …

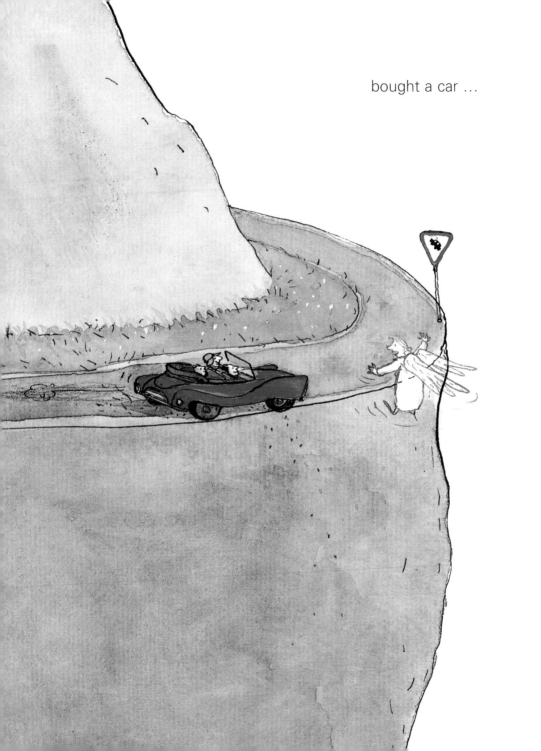

bought a car ...

became a grandfather…

All in all, it's been a good life ...

even if at times rather strange.

I've been lucky."

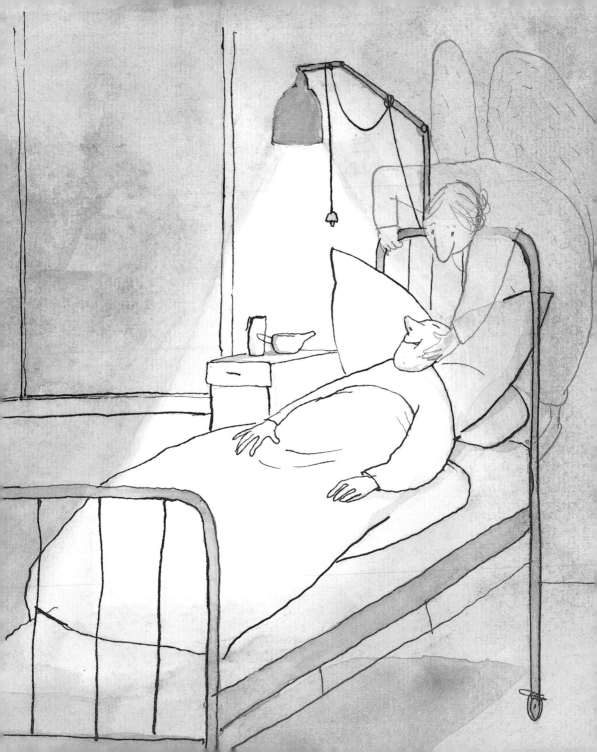

Grandpa was tired and closed his eyes.
I left quietly.

Outside, the sun was still shining.
What a beautiful day!

First published in Great Britain 2005 by Walker Books Ltd
87 Vauxhall Walk, London SE11 5HJ

2 4 6 8 10 9 7 5 3 1

Text and illustrations © CARLSEN Verlag GmbH, Hamburg 2001
First published in Germany under the title OPAS ENGEL

Published by arrangement with CARLSEN Verlag GmbH, Hamburg

English translation © 2005 Walker Books Ltd

This book has been typeset in JansonText and Univers and handlettered by the author

Printed in China

British Library Cataloguing in Publication Data:
a catalogue record for this book is available from the British Library

ISBN 1-84428-034-9

www.walkerbooks.co.uk